Keep Running, GINGERBREAD MAN

Written by Steve Smallman

Illustrated by Neil Price

QED Publishing

Once upon a time there was a little old woman and a little old man. They liked watching TV, drinking tea and eating gingerbread biscuits.

One day they baked a gingerbread man, just for a change. They gave it two raisins for eyes and sweets for buttons...

...then they popped it in the oven to cook.

But a few minutes later they heard,

"Let me out! Let me out!"

The old woman opened the
oven and out jumped the
Gingerbread Man.

Before she knew it, he was
running out of the door.

"Stop, we want to eat you!" she shouted.

The little old man and the little old woman chased
after the Gingerbread Man, but they couldn't keep up.

"Run, run as fast as you can,
You can't catch me,
I'm the Gingerbread Man!"
sang the smug little biscuit.

A cow was lying in the meadow
chewing some grass when the
Gingerbread Man ran past.

"Stop, I want
to eat you!"

shouted the cow.

She chased after the Gingerbread Man,
but she couldn't keep up.

"*Run, run as fast as you can,*
You can't catch me,
I'm the Gingerbread Man!"
sang the irritating little snack.

A horse was lazing against a fence, having a drink, when the Gingerbread Man ran past.

"Stop, I want to eat you!"

shouted the horse.

He chased after the Gingerbread Man,
but he couldn't keep up.

"*Run, run as fast as you can,
You can't catch me,
I'm the Gingerbread Man!*"
sang the annoying little teatime treat.

A fox was doing star jumps in the meadow
when along came the Gingerbread Man.

The fox chased after the
Gingerbread Man and in
no time caught up with him!

"What are you running away from?" asked the fox.

"I'm running away from the little old man, the little old woman, the cow and the horse," said the Gingerbread Man.

"They all want to eat me!"

"NO, really?" said the fox.

"You must be very fast to keep up with me!" said the Gingerbread Man.

"Well, I do try to keep fit," the fox replied.

"I walk everywhere, I play sports and I keep active! I eat well too."

"That's great," puffed the Gingerbread Man as they raced towards a fast-flowing river.

"Erm, can you swim too?"

"Of course I can swim!" said the fox.

"Then could you carry me across the river?" asked the Gingerbread Man.

"I'll fall to pieces if I get soggy!"

"No problem,"
said the fox.

"Climb onto my tail."

But as the fox swam across the river his tail started to get closer to the water!

"Quick," said the fox, "jump onto my back – it will be safer there!"

But the fox's back seemed to be
getting closer to the water!

"Quick," said the fox,
"jump onto my nose – it will be safer there!"

So the Gingerbread Man jumped onto the fox's nose...

He bounced, *then somersaulted* and soared through the air, landing on the riverbank! Then off he ran, into the sunset.

"He's a tricky little biscuit, isn't he?" wheezed the little old woman.

"We'll never catch him now!" moaned the little old man.

"Yes, you will!" said the fox, "you just need to get yourselves fit like me."

"Could you help us?" asked the cow and the horse.

"Of course!"
said the fox...

Next steps

Show the children the cover again. When they first saw it did they think that they already knew this story? How is this story different from the traditional story? Which bits are the same?

When the Gingerbread Man came to life and jumped out of the oven, how did the little old man and woman feel? Ask the children to show a shocked expression on their faces.

Why couldn't the old man and woman catch the Gingerbread Man? Why couldn't the cow or the horse catch him? The fox caught up with the Gingerbread Man easily. Why?

What did the fox do to keep himself fit? Ask the children if they enjoy exercising. What activities do they enjoy which also keep them fit?

When the fox helped the Gingerbread Man across the river, what did the children think was going to happen next? At the end of the story what did the fox do to help all of the other characters? How did this make the Gingerbread Man feel?

Have the children ever baked a gingerbread man? Ask the children to draw their own gingerbread man. What clothes and accessories are they going to give him?

Editor: Lucy Cuthew
Designer: Cathy Tincknell
Series Editor: Ruth Symons
Editorial Director: Victoria Garrard
Art Director: Laura Roberts-Jensen

Copyright © QED Publishing 2014
First published in the UK in 2014
by QED Publishing
A Quarto Group company
The Old Brewery
6 Blundell Street
London N7 9BH
www.qed-publishing.co.uk

A catalogue record for this book is available from the British Library.

ISBN 978 1 78171 651 9

Printed in China

This book belongs to:

. . . .

. . . .

04290139